{INSTA} WEDDING

A Sweet {INSTA} Novella

JEN ATKINSON

For Syd
Who really wanted Dean and Iris to get married.

Also by Jen Atkinson

Sweet RomComs

Am I 30 Yet?

Romancing Blake

The {INSTA} Series

{INSTA} Boyfriend

{INSTA} Connection

{INSTA} Kiss

{INSTA} Family

Sweet Romance

Surviving Emma

Then Came You

Love, In Theory

The Amelia Chronicles

Knowing Amelia

Love & Mercy

Dear Kate

Because of Janie

Young Adult Romance

Paper Hearts

The Untouched Trilogy

Untouched

Unknown

Undone

{INSTA} Wedding

A SWEET {INSTA} NOVELLA

ONE

Beth

"I thought Iris hated Instagram?"

"She doesn't hate it," Ebony says, zipping the back of my bridesmaid dress. "She just doesn't love it. She gets uncomfortable with everyone knowing her business, you know?"

I feel my brows pull together—Ebony just did my makeup, so I should not be scrunching up my face... but I can't help it. "Confused. So then, why is she allowing a big-time influencer to do an Instagram live of her wedding?"

Ebony turns so that I can zip her up too. Her dress is coral and chiffon, and despite the eight-and-a-half-month pregnant belly attached to her front, it looks amazing on her. Sure, her ankles are swollen and her cheeks are a little fuller, but my best friend is a glowing little moonbeam.

"I mean, her husband-to-be is a pretty big influencer. So, there's no hate. Is hate even possible for Iris?" Ebony's eyes slip up to the ceiling—thinking.

"So, why isn't he the one getting all this exposure?"

She lifts her hair so that I can zip the top half of her zipper, but glances back at me. "This particular influencer offered to donate six figures to the Animals in Crisis Foundation in the bride's name."

"Iris doesn't care about *her name* on some check." I scoff.

"No, but she does care about the animals." Ebony turns. Now that we're both all zipped up she wants to examine me. "Bethany Barns, you are beautiful! Tate's going to forget that Hawaiian wedding getaway you have planned and insist you marry him here and now."

One corner of my mouth curls with a grin—betraying the silence I've promised Tate.

"What?"

"Nothing," I say.

"No. Not nothing. You, my friend, are a sabotaging, squirrel wrangler. So, what's with the face?"

"It's a secret."

"Yes… but it's also *me*. Your best friend forever. Your Ebony. Your—"

"You have a point. Tate can't get upset with me if it's *you* I'm telling. He understands how much I love you and how much I've missed you."

Ebony's bottom lip protrudes in a pout and her eyes fill with unshed tears. But her words aren't tender. "Now, spill."

"Well," I lean in and whisper my secret truth, "We pulled a Jet and Ebony." I realize I have given in much too quickly. But the words have been begging me to say them… maybe if I just tell Ebony…

Her brows furrow. "I have no idea what that means."

"Sure you do. We," my brows raise, "*pulled* a Jet and—"

"I heard you the first time. What does that mean?" She

sets one hand on her hip, the other rests on her protruding belly. They don't know the sex of the baby, but it's a girl. I'm certain and I'm taking bets.

A knock on the door interrupts our conversation.

"It's open!" I call.

Jet pokes his head into the small room of this cabin. "The photographer will be here in half an hour," he tells us. "I'm headed out to pick up Hazel from the groomer."

Our heads are together and my truth—spoken frankly— is on the tip of my tongue, when Jet interrupts us. We both turn to look at him.

"Thank you, honey," Ebony says.

One brow quirks on his head. "Sure. Is everything okay in here?"

"Not in front of Jet," I hiss whisper. I did promise Tate. I can't be spilling these beans to everyone. "He'll let the cat out of the bag."

"Yes," Ebony says, shuffling over to the door and setting a hand on Jet's shoulder—the man looks good in a suit. "We're all good. We'll be out soon."

Jet's eyes dart from Ebony to me, but he doesn't question—he knows us well. He leans down and presses a soft kiss to the belly of my friend. It's sincere and pretty darn sweet. I might throw up a little—it's so stinking tender. But I love these two. So, I don't vomit, I just enjoy the view. "See you in a bit," he says, shutting the door behind him.

"Why are we taking photos so early? It's noon. The wedding isn't for a couple hours." I groan. But I can't deny that the Colorado rocks and woods are beautiful. This mountaintop wedding Iris has spent months planning is going to be outstanding.

"Shush. You're avoiding the subject. Now, tell me what's going on. What does it mean to pull an *Ebony and Jet*?"

"You really don't know?" I shake my head. Pregnancy has made Ebony slower than her usual self. She is excellent at multi-tasking and at deducing. She should have this by now. I lift her left hand and tap on her wedding band.

All at once, she gasps for breath. "You went to Vegas?" She whispers. "No Hawaiian wedding?"

"Oh, we're doing the Hawaii thing. We just didn't want to wait any longer. We went to the courthouse three weeks ago."

"Three weeks?" Her eyes fill and tears spill over onto her newly made-up face.

"Eb! Don't cry. I didn't think you'd cry. You did the same thing. Besides you cannot tell soul! I would never want to hurt Tate's mom. She's never been to Hawaii and he's her only son and—" I shake out my hands, then fist them at my sides.

"I'm just so happy."

"Ah." I blow out a breath. If Ebony's crying, someone is going to ask her *why*. "Well, can you be happy a little quieter and without all the tears?"

She wraps me in a hug—it's a different kind of embrace with her baby bump between us. Not bad, just different.

Her grip on me loosens and she gives a small grunt. She hunches, holds her stomach, and her brows cinch.

"Ebony?"

She blinks up at me. "Yeah?"

"Ah… you okay?"

She stands straight and puffs out a breath. "Fine." But she doesn't look fine. There's a bead of sweat on her forehead and her face has gone red. Sure, whatever occurred is gone. But *fine*... I don't think so.

She's been acting strange all morning.

And then it hits me. I drop my eyes to that round basketball filling out her dress, then back up to her face. I play tag with her eyes and her belly two more times before asking, "Ebs, are you in labor?"

TWO

Ebony

I sit on the bed in Beth's room. I loved the idea of the wedding party all staying in this cabin together, at the very sight of the wedding. Iris really did think of everything.

Except, maybe she didn't think her sister would go into labor—up in the mountains, on her wedding day, thirty minutes away from a hospital.

But I'm not worried. These things take time. And I can handle a little pain. Besides, I am not missing my sister's wedding. Sure, that may sound a little hypocritical of me, but I can't. I can't miss it. It would break Iris's heart. And I already broke her heart when I got married without her. So, nope. *Little Peanut, you're staying in until mommy says otherwise. Got it?*

I hold another internal pep talk with Little Man. It's a boy. I know it. I can feel it. He is a tiny, perfect Jet. I finish my silent dialogue only to realize that Beth is still staring at me.

"I have studied births, Bethany. I know about things. So, stop looking at me like that."

"You are. You're in labor. We're in the mountains." She lifts the skirt of her green chiffon dress with one hand and steps closer to me. "And you are in labor." Her eyes widen. "Are you going to give birth in this cabin? Is Coco going to have to deliver?"

"Shush!" I tell her. It's not like Beth to lose it. That's the only reason I'm confessing to her. "This is going to take a while! The average first-time birth takes between twelve and twenty-four hours. I am not missing Iris's wedding so that I can lay in a hospital bed, *not* giving birth! Oh, no. I will be just fine. Besides, I've only been in labor four hours." Which would have sounded so much more convincing had I not been hit with another contraction right in that second.

"Four? Ebony! Does Jet know?" Beth asks as I hunch over, one hand on my back and breathing.

I'm starting to think that smiling couple in the Lamaze video, who breathed through pain like they were simply putting a Band-aid on a paper cut, may have been full of crap.

Still, I pretend that I'm not in pain—just like I've been doing all day long. I breathe—just like the video said and I glare up at my dearest friend. "Are you kidding? Jet doesn't know. If Jet knew, I would already be in a hospital bed. He'd be feeding me ice chips this very second."

"How long are you planning to hide this?"

I wave one hand, like we're talking about a light drizzle interrupting the wedding, and not the birth of my unborn child. "I don't know… a while."

Beth's emerald eyes blink. She's got one hand on either

side of her face. Her fingers slide down, until there is no place left for them to go. "Ebony, this is a *really* bad idea."

"Worse than the time you filled Tate's apartment with taxidermied squirrels?"

"Much worse."

"Worse than the time you danced all night long with a twenty-year-old soccer player—we both know that could have gone wrong. You could have ended up the one hitched that night."

"Oh no you don't. This is way worse than that. And Billy Boy was stone-cold sober. He never would have let that happen."

I peer at her, tilting my head and breathing—*breathing*! "He would have. And we both know it. That boy was crazy about you."

"Whatever, this is worse, Ebony! It's much, much worse! You are in—"

"Shh!" I hiss at her, just as Coco opens the door to Beth's room and slips inside. She isn't dressed in her bridesmaid gown, nope she's still in ripped-up jeans and a T-shirt.

"Guys! The best thing just happened." Coco pushes up her black-rimmed glasses with the back of her hand. Her breaths are quick and her cheeks are flushed—and she's beaming.

"Ew," Beth squeaks, zoning in on Coco's fingers. "What is on your hands?"

"Just a little blood," Coco says with a blaring grin. "There was this little fawn, just down the trail and—"

"Blood? Coco!" I roll my head back, *breathing*—and not thinking about bloody deer.

"Oh, right." Her mouth turns down in a grimace.

"Sorry, Eb. It's just, I saved her and, well, it's a really great story."

"Dress," Beth says, waving her hands about. "You need to get dressed. The photographer will be here soon, right?"

"Shoot. Right again." Coco sets one hand to her flat tummy—probably leaving blood stains on her yellow shirt. "I should probably clean up."

"You think?" I can't help the touch of snark in my tone. I'm with Bethany and in labor. It's a lethal combination.

Coco stands a little straighter. "Right. Sorry! Heading to my room!"

Bethany rounds on me the minute Coco is out of sight. "You okay?"

"Fine. I am fine." I blow out a gust of air. I believe my words. I feel mediocre. Not terrible. I can do this. "My contractions are sporadic still. They're coming every four to ten minutes. And they're nothing I can't handle. So, we should be good. Your job is to cover for me if I'm in the middle of one."

"Cover for you? I'm sorry, are we at war—you're going to run from point A to point B while I use my trusty rifle to *cover* for you?"

I roll my eyes. She is so dramatic.

"Or wait, maybe we're lying to your mom and dad about why you were out so late. Sure, you were with a boy, but I'll *COVER* for you and tell them you were with me!" Pink seeps into her cheeks and ears.

"Bethany," I say, calm as a cucumber. "Are you finished? Is this little fit of yours over now?"

She stomps one foot and huffs. "Yes."

"And—will you cover for me, *best friend*?"

Her shoulders fall, her pretty green eyes flutter, as she dead-pans, "Yes, Ebony. I'll cover for you."

THREE

Coco

The blue spaghetti strap bridesmaid dress stares at me like a guilty conscience come to life. Iris would love that I saved a fawn—she'd also gasp at the state I'm in fifteen minutes before I'm scheduled to be in Iris's room. At least I think I have fifteen minutes. I can't just wash my hands and get into this dress. I'm going to need a shower.

If I don't wash my hair, I will have plenty of time to shower, dress, and put on a little makeup. I shoot Jude a quick message before I hop into the shower. Thank goodness we have service up here. It makes me giddy that he's searching for woodland creatures with Alice… but I'm gonna need help.

> @coco.crisp.99: I'm going to need zipped in six minutes.
> @hey.jude.14: I like it when you use STAT. Can you say that again but use STAT?

@coco.crisp.99: No. Now get over here.
STAT.

I am so good. I scrub like mad and in five minutes I am free of dirt, blood, and debris. I am ready for my assistant the second he steps into the room. Thankfully, I married a very punctual man.

"Zipper," I say, facing my back to him.

"Coco!" Alice yelps. "I saw a frog, and a squirrel, and something that looked like a hamster, but Daddy says it isn't a hamster."

"Huh. Field mouse?"

"I'm pretty sure it was a hamster and BLUE has no idea what he's talking about," she says, using the code name she gave her father months ago.

I feel Jude's lips, soft and tender, press to the back of my neck before he zips up my chiffon dress. He wraps one arm around my middle, hugging my back to his chest. "You know, it's pretty rude to outshine the bride."

"Right." I laugh. "I still need to put in my contacts."

"Nah," he says. "I like the glasses."

"And put on a little makeup."

"Why? You're perfect exactly as you are."

I turn to face him. "And you are the sweetest. But Iris will flip out if this day doesn't go according to her file folder, bullet point plan. And the plan says—wear makeup so that your face is brighter on camera."

"Fine. Go. Let me know how I can help."

I take one step before he's caught me by the fingers. "We're still newlyweds—remember? You can't leave me without a kiss goodbye."

Alice leans against one of the beds and giggles. I'm

waiting for the day that she groans out an *ew* when spying one of our kisses. We aren't there yet though.

I peck his lips, but that's never quite enough for Jude. Still, we have an audience, so he's pretty chaste with our ten-second exchange.

Alice hops up once her dad releases me. "Me too! I need kisses too! We're still newlyweds too!"

I lean down to peck her cheek and she pecks mine back. "Love you, Coco Butter," she says, her tone silly but serious all at once.

I shake my head. "You two are going to make me late. Do you want me to get on Iris's bad side today?" My stomach turns a little with the thought and my head feels light—or maybe it's getting ready in record time that's made me a little dizzy. I did shower and dress in major speed mode.

"Nice try," Jude says, "but Iris doesn't have a bad side."

"Daddy's right! All her sides are sweetie pie nice," Alice chimes. "I like that Iris, a lot. In fact, we could call her Rainbow."

"She might obtain a bad side if we mess up her carefully planned wedding day," I say, forgetting my nerves and fluttering. "First look is soon and I'm supposed to be with the girls helping the bride get ready! This very second!" Forget contacts. I have time for mascara and blush.

"You're right. We'll leave you. And Coco?"

"Yes, Jude."

"I love you."

I smile, a zing runs from my fingertips to my lips. "I love you, too." *Whew*. Who knew being a newlywed could be so much fun?

Jude twirls Alice out the door, they're off to find something wonderful and exciting out in the woods. I'm not gonna lie—I wish I were going with them. But Iris gets one wedding day. And it should be just as the girl wants it.

She wants traditional, magical, and outdoorsy wondrous. She also wants all of us present for bridal prep and the first look scene. Which, by the way, *isn't* traditional, but don't tell Iris that, not unless you'd like a lecture on what is new in tradition.

I can do hair and makeup in mere minutes. My skills are impressive. Still, I'm going to be the last one there—Ebony and Beth are already in their dresses. I peek at the wall clock again—yep, I am late.

I scurry out of this cabin bedroom and run smack into the groom.

Dean holds his hands in the air, and I hit him right in the cummerbund—or at least I would have if he'd been wearing one.

"Whoa. Hey, there Coco. Almost time for the first look. You ready?"

I smirk. "Me? Are you ready? You're the one about to say, *I do*."

"I am more ready for this than anything I've ever done in my life." His dark hair is combed back with pomade, ensuring he will not be running his fingers through that carefully styled do. He looks nice and more than nice—he looks thrilled. He's got that gleam in his eyes that I saw in Jude just two months ago. "Although, between you and me. You and Jude did it right. A four-week engagement is brilliant."

I laugh. "Yeah, well, this is pretty great too."

He nods. "It's going to be perfect. Iris has thought of everything."

"She's done an amazing job. Really, the girl could be a wedding planner."

"Probably," he says. "But it could be raining fireballs. As long as Iris walks down the aisle, it's going to be the best day of my life."

I smack his arm. "I just did my makeup, Dean! Besides, I'm late getting to Iris. I'm supposed to be helping her get ready this second!"

"Then go." He grins, reminding me a little of a kid on Christmas day. "I'd rather not wait any longer than I have to." And then he's gone. Out the cabin door—finding his Dad, who I recently learned is actually his adopted dad. Dean and I have more in common than I realized.

I mentally smack myself and stop all the reminiscing. "Iris!" I hurry for the bridal suite and slip in—hoping I can go undetected.

That's awfully difficult to do when you're the first one to arrive.

FOUR

Iris

I press one hand to my hip—standing in the middle of this large bedroom in nothing but my full slip and strapless bra. I drum my fingers on my waist, trying to look fierce. But I'm not great at *fierce*.

I contemplate what fierce brows might look like… distracting myself for a moment.

I blink back to reality and find Coco in the doorway, red-faced and guilty. That's when I remember I'm supposed to be looking fierce. I'm supposed to be mad—at least a little, right?

"Hello, Coco," I say—sounding a little too much like Newman from Seinfeld. That is not who I'm trying to channel.

She grins, but it's forced, and I can see way too many of her teeth. Maybe my glare is working.

"Where are the girls? You were *all* supposed to be helping me!" I haven't seen Ebony since she did my makeup this morning.

"They aren't here? I thought for sure they would be." Coco nibbles on her bottom lip. "I found this fawn with its leg all caught up in some wire and—"

The door she leans on opens, bumping right into her backside. Beth pokes her redhead inside. "Hey," she says, her smile as large and guilty as Coco's. What is up with my wedding party? They were so focused at the rehearsal dinner last night.

Coco moves to the side, letting Beth slip inside.

"Where's Ebony?" I ask. My sister isn't here yet?

"She is directly behind me. *Directly*." Beth says in a sing-song voice. Her hands clap to her hips and she sways forward, then back. She looks breathless. I saw her earlier, she didn't have sprigs falling from her updo and now she officially does.

"Did you close the door on her then?" I ask. "Is everything okay?"

"Ab-so-tute-ly," Beth says, like she's starring in a 1960s western.

There's a small knock on the door and then Ebony opens it up—a truer smile on her face than our friends. "Hi," she says, as if we aren't on a deadline.

"Cheese and crackers, Eb! First look is in eighteen minutes."

Ebony's coral dress sways about her low, large belly as she walks toward me. "Iris," she says, taking me by both hands. "This is *your* day. *You* are the bride. There is no eighteen minutes until the photoshoot. You aren't the waiting photographer today. You are the *bride*. We all wait for *you*."

My eyes turn to slits. "You mean, I'm stuck in here waiting on all of *you*." Still, I don't hate what she said. She isn't wrong. Today, I am the bride. Somehow Ebony and

Coco beat me down the aisle, but at least Beth is still single and engaged. Her destination wedding will be magical and we'll all be there.

But today is mine. Ebony's right about that.

I blow out a sigh. "I do not have the energy to be angry with all of you for the day. So, give me a hug—I am a nervous ball of energy—and then help me, for the love of all that is cheddar! I can't get into this dress without you!"

Ebony's arms wrap around me, her belly pressing into my gut. Then, Beth and Coco follow. We are a wedding sphere of sisterhood.

"I'm so glad you're all here with me," I tell them.

Beth's still living in Seattle, almost twenty hours away. And Coco moved away two months ago. She opened up her clinic in Coeur d'Alene just last week, after spending months getting the place ready and advertising. At least Ebony is close. Denver is less than two hours away. Still, our homes are spread out. It is so nice to be together.

There's a chorus of, "I'm glad too," and "I wouldn't be anywhere else," and "I love you," all around me.

And then, thump, I am kicked in the gut by my niece. It *has* to be a girl. No doubt about it. I can feel it in my bones.

"Oof," Ebony grunts.

With my hand on her shoulders, I pull my head back to peer at her. "You okay?"

"Yeah," she laughs. "Just a tough kick. See, soccer player." She says this as if it's a "team boy" defense.

"Plenty of girls play soccer," Beth says. And we secretly fist bump. "The women's National Team is amazing."

"That's true," Ebony says, but her voice is oddly strained. "Girl power. I will raise a little boy who believes in girl power—mark my word."

"*Boy?*" I say, my distraction popped like a bubble floating in the air. "You're still on that? You can't feel it? This baby is a girl, Ebony. One hundred percent. I know it." I peer around the room looking for support. "Jet knows it!"

"Jet is only saying girl to argue with me! Besides *I* can feel that it's a boy." Eb sets one hand to her hip, the other waves away my words.

"Fatherly intuition is every bit as good as motherly."

"Not this time," she says, giving a shrug.

I breathe out a laugh, snatch my dress from the hanger and hand it over to Ebony. Then, I reiterate my point. "I know it. Jet knows it. Beth knows it. Coco—"

But Coco scrunches her nose. "Sorry, Iris. I'm with Ebony on this one. Boy. All the way."

Ebony holds up her hand and Coco slaps her open palm.

"Even Jude is guessing boy."

"Nuh-uh," I moan. "He told me girl!"

"Only because Alice was right there and he's afraid of guessing boy in front of her. The pansy."

Beth lets out a snort. "That was awesome."

"Hello, lovelies!" The door to my suite opens— reminding me that I'm still not into my wedding dress. But it's only Gramgram and Mom. "There's our girls!"

"Iris," Mom says, her eyes wide, "darling, I thought you said your wedding party would help you dress."

"She did!" Ebony pipes. "We are! We are doing it right now. See?" Ebony holds up the hanger with my A-line dress as proof.

"Little angel, Gramgram has some advice for you." Gram's hips sway as she moves her way around this crowded room to my side. "Johnny once said, *The spirit of*

June Carter overshadows me tonight with the love she had for me and the love I have for her. We connect somewhere between here and heaven." Tears fill my Gramgram's eyes. "Dean is your heaven, darling, and I knew it from the moment he first put on my dead husband's bedazzled T-shirt."

"Huh," Beth says, "I did not anticipate that ending."

Gram kisses my cheek and Mom follows after her, holding me in an embrace for a long moment before they both head outside for the groom's first look.

I blow out a puff of air, tears pricking at my eyes.

"You okay, sweetie?" Ebony asks.

I peer into my sister's sweet face. Her cheeks are rounder than normal—they are beautiful. A beautiful reminder of the addition she's giving our family. "I'm okay. I'm just really happy."

Coco sighs out a laugh. "It is the happiest day of your life."

"Seriously, Iris." Beth beams at me. "If anyone in this world deserves happiness, it's you."

I nod—too afraid to talk. The lump in my throat is a warning that my makeup could easily be destroyed in less than ten seconds. Finally, I pull in a breath and say, "Now, will someone please help me get into this contraption?"

FIVE

Beth

A t least we get Iris into her wedding dress before
Ebony smiles like a really eager alligator and says,
"Oh, this baby. I think I just peed my pants. Beth!
A little help!"

Iris lifts her brows, peering at her sister, head to toe.

"I don't see anything," Coco says, staring too.

"Trust me!" Ebony bellows. "We'll only be a minute!"
She waves me over and is out the door in two seconds flat.

"Hey!" Coco calls. "First look is in five minutes!"

With one hand on her back and her face contorted like
she just ate something awful at Freedas, Ebony paces the
hall. Her pursed lips send out puffs of air.

"Please tell me that wasn't code for my water broke," I
hiss at her.

"Not yet," she says and a moan escapes her lips.

"*Not yet?* Ebony, I don't like this. I think we need to go to
the hospital."

I swear, smoke and steam and an angry haze exits my

best friend's ears. "We are going nowhere! Don't challenge me on this, Beth. I *will* take you down with me."

"What is this, fight club? Ebony! You. Are. In. Labor."

"This *is* fight club. It is. And I win. So are you with me or are you the loser?"

"Geez. You are an angry laboring lady, aren't you?" I rub my fingers over the ache sprouting on my forehead. "I already said I'm with you. But I'd like to go on record saying I also think this is a lousy idea."

"What's a lousy idea?" Half of Coco's body pokes from the door. "You guys running off on the bride? Why yes, that is a bit lousy."

"We aren't running off," I say, darting a glance at Ebony. I did tell her I was all in. We're hiding her labor, not saving her dignity. "Ebony had to change her panties."

Coco's nose wrinkles. "Ew."

"Ew? Did you just say *ew*? Miss I-stuck-my-entire-arm-up-a-cow's-yoo-hoo is saying *ew* because I need new undies?" Ebony's face is cherry red and her eyes stare daggers at our friend.

"Ah… *Sorry?*" Coco says, but it comes out more like a question. Coco pushes up the rim of her glasses. "I'm grabbing the bouquet. You two need to head back in there. You're making Iris anxious."

"We wouldn't want that," I say—and I just can't seem to hide the sarcasm in my voice.

"No," Ebony is perfecting the art of glaring this weekend, "we wouldn't."

"You two need a vacation. I think you're working too hard." Coco purses her lips, and then she heads down the hall.

I watch her go, passing a couple on the way—their arms around one another.

Wait—

"Granddad?" I yip. Is that my granddad—nuzzling Ebony's grandmother's neck?

"Oh, hey there, Dolly."

"Gramgram?" Ebony squeaks, following my gaze.

Georgia lifts her head. "Oh, hello darlings. Frank and I were just heading out for the first look. Need anything?"

"A bucket," I whisper. "I may need a bucket."

"Holy insta pot! What are you two up to?" Ebony barks —at least her pains are gone.

"I just told you, we're headed outside. Don't make us wait long," Gramgram says, taking my granddad by the hand and leading him out the front door.

"What's going to happen if we make them wait too long?" I stare ahead, unblinking, trying my darndest not to picture the nuzzling.

"Oof," Ebony moans, one hand on her stomach— bringing me back to the present.

I peer at my friend. "We aren't going to get away with this."

"Yes, we are," she growls.

Just past my friend, through the window, I see a tall bearded hottie walking outside on the deck.

"Tate!" I yip—unable to hide the grin that my new husband produces. He's just what I need. "Honey!"

"Honey?" Ebony says, her tone full of mockery.

"I'm allowed. We're married."

Tate rounds the corner of the outside entrance. Whew, that man is a tall drink of water. And I am thirsty.

"Hey," he says, wrapping one arm around my waist. His

beard and lips nuzzle at my neck and I can't even help the swoony sigh that falls from my chest.

"Holy mackerel, and you said I was pathetic." Ebony puffs out a breath, one hand on her stomach, the other arched to support her back.

Tate lifts his head with her criticism.

But I don't care. She can talk all she wants.

Until she says—"You look a little like your granddad and my gramgram just now."

I pause—mid-nuzzle. "Hey. *Newlyweds*. We're allowed."

Tate blinks, peering down at me. "I thought we weren't telling anyone."

I lift one shoulder. "But it's Ebony."

"Yeah, it's *me*, Tate." She gives him a sympathetic smile.

"Right." He nods. He's stupidly adorable. Was he always this adorable? "It's just—we don't want it getting back to my mom."

"No way," Ebony says. "It won't. I'm a vault. All locked up."

Tate clears his throat. "Yes…"

"You don't believe me?" she says. I'm not sure Tate understands what he's dealing with right now. He knows sweet, smart, competitive Ebony. But he hasn't met the monster living inside this laboring woman.

"I do. It's just—you *are* the person who told me that Beth doesn't lock up until nighttime. You know, so I could sneak into her house."

"I was helping you, Tate!" Ebony guffaws. "See if I ever do that again. I *should* tell your mother you ran out and got married without her!"

"Whoa!" I say, playing the ref. I hold up one hand. "Yo,

pot. Remember me? I'm the kettle. Let's *not* tell Tate's momma anything she doesn't need to know."

"Beth—" he starts, but I cut him off.

"It's fine. It's all fine. Ebony knows. It's okay. Guess what? Ebony is in labor. Now you know her secret too."

"Bethany!" Ebony screeches. Then, I am shoved in the shoulder by my very pregnant bestie.

"He's my *husband*! Husbands don't count. I'm allowed to tell Tate everything."

"Labor?" Tate swallows. "Like actual labor?"

"Yep. No biggie. Except we aren't telling Jet or Iris—so mums the word, babe." I kiss his cheek and pat him on the behind—sending him on his way. One crisis at a time.

Only Tate doesn't go along his way. "Wait. Are you telling me we aren't going to the hospital?"

"Right," Ebony nods.

"And that Jet doesn't know?" Tate's eyes skirt from Ebony to me.

"Exactly." Another pat to his bottom—because it's time to move on, but mostly, I just really like that man's butt. "Now you're all caught up."

"Besties and hubbies don't tell. Right, Tate?" Ebony says —the monster inside of her is ready to rear its head once more. "You don't tell Jet my secret and I won't tell your mother yours."

"Bethany," he says, sounding a whole lot like Ebony did just two minutes ago. He pulls me by the elbow so that we're on the other side of the door. Alone. "What are we doing here?"

"Ebony refuses to stop Iris's wedding. She doesn't want to ruin anything. So, the best thing we can do is push everything along. The quicker we get Iris married, the faster I can get her to the hospital."

Tate palms himself in the face. "If you ever go into labor and not tell me so we can attend a wedding, I'm investing in taxidermy classes and stuffing a creature for you for every single holiday."

"Oh, baby. If I hid it, you would never ever know." I press a soft kiss to his lips, then pat that butt again for good measure.

SIX

Ebony

I'm not worried. Nope. I'm great. Nothing to see here folks. Just a girl having contractions every ten minutes. No biggie.

"Beth," I groan when she meets me back in the hall. "I can't believe you told Tate!"

Beth types on her phone—ignoring me.

"Are you DMing your husband?"

She blinks, peering up at me. "Shh! We aren't using the H word until after Hawaii. I thought you could keep a secret!"

"I thought *you* could!" I roar back at her.

She takes one step closer. "Husbands don't count!" Her whisper is simultaneously a yell.

"Stop using the H word!" I tell her. That's right, follow your own rules, Bethany Barns. I glimpse down at her phone. "Hey—what is that? What are you googling? Bethany—give me that."

She holds the phone to her chest.

"How many times did I hand my phone over to you when I first met Jet?"

"More than you should have," she says.

"That's right. Now, hand it over. I thought—"

Beth slaps her phone into my palm and I peer down at the screen.

"Beth! Why are you googling how to deliver a baby in the woods."

"Oh, I don't know, because that's what I'll be doing in an hour."

"Stop," I tell her. "We're going to be fine. Now, shhh!"

She scolds me just in time—Coco is back, walking toward us, bouquet in hand.

I stuff Beth's phone into my armpit.

"Hey, you guys are still out here? Are you done being weird yet?"

I swallow. Oh, how I wish I could say yes. But I'm pretty sure I'm gonna be acting a little strange up until the minute this baby decides to exit my body. "Weird? You're weird." I laugh and Beth fakes a laugh with me.

Coco smirks. "Are you coming?"

"Soon," I nod and watch as Coco heads back into Iris's room without us. But between Gramgram and Tate we've been out here way too long. Too long for Iris and too long for my contracting body.

Then, the outside door fills with my favorite person on the planet—and the last person I want to see. Jet knows me too well. He will figure me out if I'm not careful.

He waves through the window, then opens the door, Hazel on a leash beside him.

"Honey!" I yelp, my tone too high to be natural.

"Hey, baby." Jet's warm hand cups my cheek. He leans

down, placing a kiss on my temple. "Hazel's back from the groomer and ready to be the flower girl—or whatever Iris is calling her."

"Oh! Jet!" I shake my head. "You—you can't see the bride before the wedding!"

He smirks, his brows pulled together. "Why not?"

"Yeah, why not?" Beth says—to which I elbow her.

"Because!" I say.

"Right," Beth clears her throat. "Because it's an old… Johnny Cash rule. No brothers-in-law before the ceremony." She lifts one shoulder, pulling a face. "Crazy, I know. You're the one who married into this family, not me."

"Johnny Cash tradition? Iris is doing this?"

I blow out a sigh. The most ridiculous story in the world —and he's believing it. "Yes. For Gramgram. You know how close they are. Gramgram was pretty insistent and Iris, well Iris went along with it." My ten minutes are almost up. I can feel it, in my bones, in my back, and in the tightness of my belly. "So, honey, you have to leave. I mean, not too far. I want to know where you are—at all times, actually—but I just can't see you."

"I thought the bride couldn't see me? Wait. Isn't that the groom? The groom can't see the bride."

"That's not Johnny Cash's rule!" Beth bellows. She knows just as well as I do that my time has to be coming to an end.

"But you aren't the bride." He holds one hand toward me.

"But she'll be with the bride and we're already late! Geez, Jet!" Beth cries. "Are you trying to ruin Iris's day?"

"Ah." His thick brows pull together. "No. I just picked up the dog. I—"

"Thanks. We'll take her from here." Then Beth pats his back like a two-year-old, sending him on his way.

Jet glimpses behind him, peering back at me, confusion in his eyes.

"Bye, sweetie. See you at the ceremony." I wave, then suck in a breath, just as another contraction hits.

SEVEN

Coco

I bend down to give Hazel a love. She's such a sweet pup. She is Iris in dog form. "She looks great."

"She does." Iris crouches in her wedding gown, scratching her dog behind the ears. Hazel licks her chin and Iris doesn't wince or worry one bit about her makeup.

A tap on the door must mean Beth and Ebony have decided to join us once more. What in the world is up with those two? They let the dog inside, but then they never made an appearance.

I open the door—wondering why they don't just enter themselves—but it isn't Ebony and Beth. It's a woman in a purple suit, her blue ruffled shirt bushing out at the collar.

"Hey there," she says, flicking one of her black braids from her shoulder.

"Ah—"

Iris pokes her head around me. "Yara." She dabs her lips together, smoothing out her lipstick. "Hi."

"We're all set up for the groom's first look. You ready?" Yara grins, her white teeth bright.

"I'm sorry. Who are you?" I say. Ebony isn't here, and neither is Beth. They both would act as protectors and Iris clearly isn't comfortable. So, protector is now my job.

"I'm the influencer donating six figures to the animal charity of Iris's choice. Animals in Crisis, right, Iris?"

My friend gives a small smile. "Yes. That's right."

"We're set to go live, whenever you're ready."

"Live," Iris gives me wide eyes. "Exciting."

"Or we could just record it, and post it later?" I suggest, but Yara shakes her head.

"We have people waiting. No, we've promised a live event for Dean's living-out-loud followers." Yara sets a hand to her plum waist, her eyes back on my friend. "See you soon, Iris?"

Iris nods. "I'll be the one in white."

A chortle leaves Yara's mouth and she waves, exiting the room.

"Iris, you don't have to do this," I tell her—but in my head, I'm yelling for Ebony to get back here! Where is that girl?

"I do. I've already said I would. Besides, do you have any idea how many animals will be helped, all because I let a few people see me on my wedding day?" Iris runs a hand down the lace and tule of her dress. "Now, where's my matron of honor?"

"I'll find her. She probably had to pee again."

Iris sighs. "Maybe."

I reach out a hand and Iris takes mine. "Don't worry about anyone but Dean. You're stunning, by the way. The most beautiful bride I've seen. You're going to break the internet with that kind of beauty."

I kiss my friend's cheek and hurry back into the hall. Rather than search the cabin high and low for Ebony and Beth, I call Ebony's cell.

Voicemail.

So, I call Beth.

"Hey, there chicka-tee-ta."

"Bethany! Where are you guys?"

"On our way."

"Where are you this second?" I have been living with a six-year-old for the last two months, I can step into mom mode when I need to.

"Hall bathroom, but we're on our way."

I tap on the hall bathroom door. "You're not *on your way*. I know that because I'm here. And you didn't even meet me a quarter of the way."

Beth pushes the door ajar just a few inches. But it's enough. Ebony's in the tub. Red-faced and sweaty.

"Cheese and crackers," I say, mimicking Iris. I push my way in, though Beth attempts to stop me. "Labor? You're being a lame weirdo because you're in labor? Ebony!"

"It isn't my fault," she says with a puff. "Talk to Peanut." Her fingers grip the edge of the tub and she glares at me. *Whew*, she's got that parent scowl down. Peanut won't be getting away with anything.

"We have to get you to the hospital."

Beth shakes her head—is she insane? Have all of the marbles fallen out of her red head?

"I will not wreck Iris's wedding!" Ebony's grip on the tub lightens, the contraction must be passing. "This child is going to stay inside of my body until his aunt is wed! Got it, Peanut?"

"Besides, you're here. You've delivered lots of babies," Beth says like me being a veterinarian fixes everything.

"Animal babies! I've never delivered a human baby. What if something were to go wrong? She needs a doctor, a hospital, a—"

"Plenty of people have home births," Ebony says, both her hands on the outer edge of the tub. She stands up, lifting one leg over the edge of the tub. "And they're fine. Peanut is a good boy."

"Except that he's a *she*," Beth sings.

"No. You agree with me, Coco, right?" Ebony says, on the outside of the tub, now.

"Does it matter? I can't believe you're going along with this Beth."

"Oh, she's good." One side of Beth's lip curls upward. "She's very good. She wouldn't listen to a logical word I said."

"Coco," Ebony says, her tone smooth and sleek. "This is Iris. *Our* Iris. Our sweet girl who does everything for everyone else."

I think of the animals she's saving—she's going *live* on the biggest day of her life, something she hates—all to help who knows how many four-legged creatures.

"This is her day. She gets one. Let's give it to her. I can't make it about me."

I press both fists into my eye sockets. "Grr. How far apart are the contractions?"

"Ten minutes," Ebony says. "Give or take a little. See? We aren't even close to being ready. My doctor said to come to the hospital when they are five minutes apart."

"I'm guessing your doctor wouldn't say hang out in the woods all day while we wait for them to get five minutes apart, now would he?"

"Ooo," she sings. "You agree—this could take *all day* long. See? What's the point in putting a stop to Iris's day when I won't have this kid for hours?"

I sigh and rub at my temples. "You're right, Beth. She's *very* good."

EIGHT

Iris

———

I practice the meditation breathing that Dean taught me and pat the top of Hazel's head. *In then out.* Breathe in the daisies and blow away the petals.

"Hey," a soft voice says. Ebony's voice.

I blink, my eyes open to find all three members of my bridal party lined up and peering down at me. Beth grins, her red hair spilling over the top of her emerald green dress I picked for her. Coco's hands are clasped in front of her cornflower blue dress, her eyes teary as she looks down at me. Ebony's coral pink chiffon gown rolls over her baby belly like a waterfall. A tear slips down my sister's cheek and she swipes it away, her smile wide.

"Are you ready?"

I forget that they've all been all over the place today because mostly, they've always been there for me. I adore the three of them and that's what comes to mind now. I love them. I love Dean. And today, we're all together, with our family and friends—and Yara of course. But even that makes me happy. All that money is going to a good cause and at the end of the day, the only thing that really matters is being here—in our happy place, with the ones we love. After today, we'll forever be *we* instead of he and I.

"Somebody lace me up," I say, lifting my dress to where my white Converse sit on my feet. I'm not sure I could bend over in this contraption to tie my shoes. "I am so ready."

The three exchange looks and Coco kneels down to tie my tennies. Finished, Coco stands and Ebony holds out her hand to help me up. "He's waiting."

I blow out a breath. "Is it strange to be nervous to see the one person who you feel the most at home with?"

"It's your wedding day," Coco says, walking to the door and opening it up for me. Hazel trots after her, waiting by the door as if she knows it's time.

"I was a ball of nerves," Beth sighs, lifting one shoulder, her gaze zoning. Her head pops up like one of those wack-a-mole games and her eyes have suddenly forgotten how to blink. "I WILL be a ball of nerves. *Will.* Future tense. How could I know? I mean, I don't. Because I am single and ready to mingle. Well, not mingle. I love Tate. But super single over here." She holds up her left hand, wiggling her engagement ring at us.

"Beth, did you get married without us? And then forget to tell us about it?" Coco rests one hand on her hip.

"No," she moans, her voice shrill and abnormal. "I will see you all in Hawaii!"

"You two." Coco points from Ebony to Beth, then shakes her head.

I'm pretty sure Beth *is* married—and I *am* the last one to make it to the altar. That's all right—Gramgram would say that *they saved the best for last. That I was Johnny's choice. That dessert comes at the end of the meal.* Or something equally witty and confusing. Either way, I am rolling with words that Gramgram didn't, but could have said. I'm gonna let them lead me all the way out of this cabin and over that mountain floor where I will see Dean for the first time today.

We step outside and into the sunshine, where Gramgram, Mom, Dad, and the rest of our friends and family wait. Yara stands ahead of us all, her phone directed my way. I pretend she's just another guest and not videoing my live reaction for the entire world to see.

Nope, instead, I scan over to where Jet, Tate, and Jude stand to the side next to a quaking aspen. Jude smiles and Tate waves. But my brother-in-law—who I really do love like a brother—has his back turned to me. Jet is facing the mountain—not me.

Ebony and Beth aren't the only ones acting off today.

We walk past the guys and Jet leans to the side and whispers to Bethany. "Can I look now?"

"No! Gramgram is watching you, Jet Jacobson."

I peer back at my brother-in-law, his suit jacket back still facing me. "Why is Gramgram watching Jet?" I whisper to Ebony.

"Oh, you know. She doesn't want him to get too excited. No one needs Jet out of hand."

My brows lower, I study her, trying to make out the words she's said. None of them make sense. We walk across the dirt and pine needle ground—and I'm thankful for my Converse. Who would choose heels on a day like today? At least here.

"Iris," Ebony nods and I follow her gaze.

There he is. My Dean. His back is turned and he's waiting for me. Hazel sees him too. She leaves my side and runs over to where he stands, sitting next to him and butting her head to his thigh. He reaches down, giving her a sweet hello. His shoulders rise and fall with breath.

I'm not the only one anxious.

I lift up my skirts and pick up the pace.

Ebony chuckles, lagging behind. "Don't mind me. I don't want to hold you back."

Yara and two of her helpers walk off to the side, but they keep in step with me just fine, her phone points in my direction. "Iris," Yara says before I can reach my spot, right behind Dean. "Anything you want to say to Instagram? They've been rooting for you and Dean since they learned about you. We're live."

Sure, that last bit of info makes me want to vomit. Or possibly knock Yara's phone right out of her hand. But I'm not going to cause a scene and ruin this day. I agreed to her being here. I didn't know I'd be talking to the Instagram world, though.

"Eighty-seven thousand people are watching," she says with a smile.

My head feels light. Eighty-seven *thousand?*

"Ahh—" Okay, maybe I will be making a fool of myself —live.

Ebony's hand, so familiar and loving finds mine. She gives it a squeeze and my senses return.

I should tell everyone to go adopt a pet. I should tell everyone watching to be extra kind today. I should say something profound and important with so many eyes on me. Instead, I tilt my head and give a one-shoulder shrug. "Time to see my groom." I wave and go back to pretending that Yara is just Dean's funny cousin whom I've never met until today.

"Right here," Ebony whispers, taking me by both hands. She pats one side of my updo and straightens out one of the strings of hair falling about my face. "The most beautiful bride to ever walk the aisle," she tells me. She backs up, standing with our parents and Gramgram who've all trailed behind me here. Mom and Gram are already crying and the ceremony hasn't even begun. Dad winks at me, one hand in his pocket. Hazel barrels over, from Dean to me, sitting to the left of me. Dean's mom and dad stand just past him and Melissa covers her mouth when she sees me. Anson dabs at his eyes, and with everyone else crying, I figure I don't need to. My heart is going to burst.

"Turn around Dean Hale!" I say with a chuckle.

"Can I?" Dean asks, fisting and shaking his hands at his sides.

"Yes!" Melissa calls.

"Come on Dean! Walk that line!" Gramgram yells from behind me.

Dean turns. His blue eyes start at my full skirt and climb to my waist, my chest, then my eyes.

"Iris," he says, my name a prayer.

"Hey, Dean Cooper Hale. Wanna share your last name with me today?"

He sniffs and laughs and brushes a straying tear from his eyes. I like this new tradition. Who needs to wait for the altar for that first kiss anyway? I pick up my skirt and meet him in the middle of this mountain floor.

"Love you more," he says, wrapping one arm around me.

"Love you most," I tell him, ignoring our audience—including the eighty-seven thousand sets of stranger's eyes that peek in on this moment. I push up on my toes and

Dean pulls me close, his nose grazing mine before his lips claim me. My mouth parts and I kiss him back as if my Gramgram weren't standing ten feet away watching the whole scene.

"Save some for the actual ceremony!" Beth calls.

"Walk that line," Gramgram shouts.

"Gram," I hear Jet say. "Am I allowed to see the bride yet?"

With so many voices, the real world all comes back in an instant.

An Instagram instant. "Yes!" Yara says. "I couldn't have written that better. We'll be back on for the ceremony. But you've got a break until then."

I clear my throat and peck my intended once more, quick and chaste. I lean my head against his chest, his heart pounds every bit as erratic as mine.

"Look boy, look. What do I care if you look or not?" I hear Gramgram say behind me, her tone impatient.

Jet turns, looking at me. One eyebrow quirks as he sees Dean and I together. Then his eyes dart to our redheaded friend. "Bethany?"

"Jokes! Ha! We got you, Jacobson!" Beth points at Jet with both hands.

Jet doesn't laugh. He tilts his head. His narrowed eyes rove over to Ebony who gives him a wary grin and a shoulder shrug.

But I don't have time to dwell on whatever Jet and Beth are teasing about.

"Iris," Mom calls. "Time for pictures."

NINE

Beth

W e've taken four group wedding party photos—
Iris giving her photographer posing tips in the
kindest possible way—when Ebony latches
onto my arm.

"Bathroom!" she bellows. "Pregnant lady needs the
restroom."

"Ah, we could do just groom and his men?" Sadie, the
photographer suggests.

Ebony pulls me along after her, holding her belly and
squeezing the guts out of my forearm. I'm pretty sure she
doesn't have to pee.

"Ebony," Jet calls, jogging up behind us. "Baby, you
okay?"

"Mm-hmm." She hums, but she isn't okay. I know it. Jet
knows it. The skin that used to cover my forearm knows it.

"Hey, Jet," Dean calls from Sadie's prime lighting spot—
err, at least the lighting spot that Iris prompted her to use. "I
need my groomsmen!"

"That's you!" I tell Jet. I give him a nod, feeling a little bad for the poor chump. "I've got her," I tell him and then I pray with all my might that it's true. *I promise to never buy another taxidermied squirrel—at least with the intention of torture. Just let me be able to take care of my friend.*

We barely make it inside for Ebony to slip down onto the cabin's living room couch. She huffs and puffs like she's possibly trying to blow a house down. Does that make me a little pig?

"Hey," says a voice from the door, making Ebony and I both jump in our spots. "We okay in here?" Coco pokes her head inside, then peeks back out.

"How much time do we have?"

Coco studies the photo taking just outside this cabin. "I'd say ten minutes, give or take. But then, I'm not the photographer."

Ebony squeaks out a cry, her cheeks puffed.

"Eb," Coco says and in my head I picture her talking to a llama in that same voice. "Just breathe, sweetie. You got this. Breathe through it." Coco crouches next to her.

Oh, mama. This is getting real. Too real.

"Check her!" I say to Coco.

"Check her?"

"Yes! You know, see if she's dilated. There has to be a ruler around here somewhere."

"Beth," Coco stands and sets a soft hand on my shoulder. "Sweetie. You're losing it. I'm not *checking* her."

"Don't you want to be checked, Eb?" My jaw clenches. Coco is right. I have got to pull it together. But Ebony has got to quit puffing like that! It's freaking me out.

Ebony shakes her head no.

"Your water hasn't broken, right?" Coco's back at

Ebony's side. I sit on the other—pulling in my own calming breaths.

"No," Ebony says, tears on her cheeks. "I'm sorry, Beth. That one was rough. The next one isn't going to be that bad."

"I'm not sure that's how this works. Isn't this kind of a progressive operation?" I clamp my top teeth onto my bottom lip, studying her.

"Peanut told me so," Ebony growls. "It's going to be better next time."

I blink, then slide my glance to Coco. I don't know what to say to that. I'm not the only one who has lost it.

"We need a plan, Ebony. An *exit* plan. I know you want Iris to have her day, but you want your baby safe too, right?"

"Of course," Ebony gives off another breathy rumble and glares at our friend.

"Right. So, we need a plan. It's a thirty-minute drive into town. How far apart are your contractions?" Coco is the coolest and the calmest of us all. She's amazing. She's Wonder Woman. No wonder Jude married her after a four week engagement. She's like a fabulous goddess and I love her.

"Eight minutes, sometimes nine."

"And," I say, regaining my composure, "sometimes, seven."

"Your water hasn't broken." Coco just needs a white jacket and a chart to mark on and I'll give her all the money in my bank account to do this job. "So, we have some time. But Ebony, if the contractions get to five minutes apart we have to go."

"Four," Ebony says, bargaining with her.

"This isn't a used car lot, Ebony!" I say, both hands on my hips.

But apparently, it is, because Coco nods. "Fine. We go once your contractions are four minutes apart *or* your water breaks—that one is non-negotiable."

Ebony holds out her hand and they shake on it.

"Until then—" I start, but Ebony stops me with a glare.

"We stick to the plan," She says. "Jet and Iris stay in the dark and while I'm contracting, we deflect." Ebony holds out a hand, wiggling her fingers, ready for someone to help her get to her feet.

"Coco!" Alice Taylor, Coco's stepdaughter is heard before she's seen. "Daddy says it's time for pictures. Time to get this show on the road!"

Coco stands, leaving me to take care of Ebony. "Hey, sweet pea! It's time for the girls to get their picture taken?"

"Yep! And Iris said I get to stand by Hazel since I'm the one walking her down the aisle."

"Sweet! Let's go."

Alice slips her hand into Coco's and they're gone.

"You ready?" I ask Ebony. Her hand sits in mine, her bottom still on the couch cushion but she stares past me to where Coco and Alice just stood.

Her eyes are filled to the brim—I'll never get used to Ebony McCoy crying. "Coco's like a *mom*, Beth."

"She is."

Ebony blows out one last tired breath. "I'm ready. Like Alice said, let's get this show on the road."

TEN

Ebony

I only have to leave two more times during the photoshoot. I head back to the cabin, sweating like an unsheared llama in ninety-degree heat. Really, I'm just a laboring pregnant lady trying to walk from here to there. Still, I'm glad this dress doesn't have sleeves or I'd be leaving a mark.

Iris and Dean have their own planned photo shoot before the guests arrive. So I have a minute.

The living room is crowded and I don't need an audience. I head back to my room, but I'm followed. How did I miss Jet right on my heels? Wasn't Beth supposed to distract? Where's the team?

"Ebony," my husband calls. "Sweetie, you okay?"

"Stop asking me that!" I bark, rather than blatantly lie to the man. I am *not* okay. I have a baby attempting to escape my body when it isn't time. It isn't time, Peanut!

"Sorry, you just seem off." Despite my harsh tone, he

wraps one arm around my shoulders, pulling me close and making me sure that the world is right once more.

"I *am* off. I've been off for nine months." I press my face into his chest, letting him guide me into our room. "I bet you can't wait for your real wife to return."

"My real wife? Are there two of you?"

I smirk—not finding this funny. "Sort of. The woman you fell in love with and then this beast who can't stop blubbering."

"Hey, now. Be kind, that beast is my wife." Jet runs a hand down my temple and cheek, tipping my chin upward.

I flutter my eyelids closed and wait for landing. Jet Jacobson does not disappoint. Man, that boy can kiss.

"Better?" he says, the tip of his nose brushing mine.

I blink up at him, at his tan face and glorious eyelashes. My heart beats a little calmer. "I love you, Jet."

His mouth curves into a grin and he pecks another kiss to my lips.

I breathe—like a regular human being. At least for the next thirty seconds.

Yep, I walked deep into that rabbit hole called *denial*.

"I need you to get Beth," I say as pain shoots through me.

"Beth?"

"Mm-hmm." I wave a hand at him and sit on the bed. "It's wedding related. Go." I try to smile, but it's hard with my jaw clenched.

"Sure. Ceremony's in less than an hour, you good? Ebony?"

I am not good.

"I'm hot… and this dress... And—just Beth. Get Beth." I fist the quilt on this bed, but keep myself together—until Jet leaves. I lay back and whimper, breathing through the tightness and the pain. "Peanut. Your timing is awful. Please. Just give Mama two hours." The ceremony should be over by then—right?

I breathe and count, and focus. Screwing up my face to look perfectly normal when the door creaks open.

"Ebony?" Beth says, her tone softer than usual.

"Where's Jet?"

"I sent him and Tate on an errand." She twists her wrist, peering down at her smartwatch. "How long has it been going?"

"Three minutes."

She nods—but her eyes are a little wider than normal. "That's a long one."

"I have a plan."

"I know. I was there. Coco's plan. Five minutes—"

"Four," she corrects, snatching onto my elbow.

"Right. Four minutes or water breaking."

"And," she says, "we're going to move this wedding right along. You talk to the reverend. I've heard she can get long-winded. Let her know that Iris and Dean don't need a big show."

"But their wedding is literally a show. Yara's here filming—"

"Quick and sweet. You tell her!" I swallow and shut my eyes, resting while Peanut allows me to. "Then, get Coco and Tate on seating duty. I want everyone in their seats in the next twenty minutes. Got it?"

"Ebony—it's possible some guests won't even be here yet."

"Everyone important is already here! Show on the road!" I say, repeating little Alice. "Let's get going!" I clap my hands. "I mean that singular, as in *you* go. I'm gonna lay down for a while."

"Right. You got it. What do you need me to do?"

I puff out a breath—so so tired. "Beth, most of all, if anything goes wrong, I need you to help me make it right. Okay? We can make it through the ceremony. I know we can."

She nods her pretty little redhead. "We've made it this far."

ELEVEN

Coco

"Do you think Jet and Ebony will name their baby after me? I mean, I just sat Uncle Ivan in his seat like a champ. I gave that old man no other choice. He wanted a drink—*nope*—too bad. All for *the cause*," Tate, Beth's fiancé or husband, I'm not really sure at this point, whispers the last two words as he waves more guests into their seats.

I chuckle and press a hand to my fluttering stomach. "Why wouldn't they name him after you? That makes more sense than naming your children after your life-long favorites. That's what my mother did." I lift one brow, thinking about my mom, Lucy. She named all of us kids after her favorite things in life—including her childhood dog. That's right, my brother's name is Cooper, after a pet our mom had growing up. So—anything is possible. "Hey Tate, have you seen Alice?"

My stepdaughter might be my favorite human on the planet—well, right next to her dad.

"She's sitting with Ebony's grandma and Frank. I think she's getting more of an education than Jude bargained for when he set that up."

"Gramgram is harmless." I bite my cheek. "Mostly. Though chances of Alice coming home with a diehard love for Johnny Cash are very real. How do you think Jude feels about the man in black?"

"Ah—" Tate doesn't get to answer though.

"Wow," Dean says, walking past us. "We are really filling up. We only have two rows of seating left. I know Iris had us set up extra chairs—just in case."

"That's right," I say, smiling at my friend. "Looks like you're going to get a jump on those vows."

"Iris has a plan—"

"And everything is going according to plan—even better than planned." I nod at the groom, nerves blooming in my gut again. "Go find your spot! We might be able to start early!"

Tate and I watch as Dean walks down the path to where he and Iris will stand. He stops and says hello along the way, but he's going. He's getting there.

"Do you think he's suspicious?

"He's about to get married." I laugh. "He's got bigger things on his mind."

"That's true."

I squint. "Did you and Beth have a secret wedding?"

Tate coughs—on nothing, then clenches his jaw. "Did Beth say we had a secret wedding?"

"No," I say, trying to read his expression.

"Then no, we didn't."

I shake my head—I think he's lying. "Go find your place. I'll grab the girls."

I head to Ebony's room first—we're giving Iris a united front. That's the least we can do. I open the door a smidgen and squeeze my way inside. Beth sits on the bed next to Ebony, patting her forehead down with a damp cloth. Her face is pale, but her cheeks are pink.

"How many minutes apart?" I ask, praying I did the right thing by letting Ebony stay at the wedding.

"Six," Beth tells me—to which Ebony glares at her.

"Six and a half. It was closer to seven."

Beth licks her lips. "No, it wasn't." One of her red brows quirks upward. She isn't afraid of a fight. But I'm pretty sure she's terrified of delivering her best friend's baby.

"We've got everyone in their seats. We're ready to get the bride." I hold a hand out to my friend.

"Ebony!" Beth says, her tone panicked. "What are we going to do in six minutes when a contraction hits? Huh? What's the plan? I need to know."

Ebony lays her hand in mine and I pull her to her feet. "You made a promise, Bethany Barns or whatever your name is now. If something goes wrong, *you're* fixing it."

"But how?" Beth's got both hands on her green chiffon hips. She shifts from her left foot to her right.

"That's your job to figure out," Ebony tells her. "And I have faith in you."

But I don't know what she thinks Beth will do. She's got all her little chicky eggs in Beth's terrified basket.

"Let's go," Ebony says, walking to the door. "Clock's ticking."

She's faster than I thought she'd be.

We tap on Iris's door across the hall.

"Ready? It's time," Ebony says peering in at Iris.

We're twelve minutes ahead of schedule. Beth had her

chat with the reverend and Tate and I have everyone seated. Still—I sort of expect Iris to object. To stick to her carefully planned schedule.

Iris's mom peers up at the clock on the wall, but Iris stands, ready to go.

"Dean's in place," I say before Mrs. McCoy can bring anything up. "And your dad is waiting just outside the cabin door."

"Then, let's go get married," Iris says, her smile blaring. "Well, it's too late for the rest of you—you already are."

"Hey, shhh!" Beth groans, "I never said that."

Next to her, Ebony laughs, then hunches, whimpering in pain.

"Hey!" Beth bellows. "Did you see that taxidermied deer head on the way in? It's fantastic work!" She's yelling. She's fixing all Ebony's problems—any way she knows how. "Let me show you!" She snatches Iris by one arm and Mrs. McCoy by the other, charging for the exit.

"I'm not really interested," Mrs. McCoy says.

"It's on our way!" Beth sings, walking the two out the door.

"You might owe her for the rest of time, you know that right?" I say to a contracting Ebony.

"Believe me," she groans, "she owes *me*."

Another minute passes, then Ebony and I meet them at the cabin exit. Our bridesmaid music already in play.

TWELVE

Iris

I watch as everyone leaves the cabin, Ebony giving me a little wink as she goes. She looks tired—maybe an outdoor wedding where my very pregnant sister has to hike all over the place wasn't the best idea.

"Iris, stop stressing," Dad tells me, taking my arm and looping it through his.

"How do you know I'm stressing?"

"You've got that line down the center of your forehead. Just like your mother." He taps his finger on his own head. His eyes—blue, like mine—rove over my face.

"Ebony looks tired. A mountaintop wedding may not have been the best plan for her. She's probably walked five miles today."

"She's fine. Besides, we're here. No going back now." Dad shrugs, smiling down at me. "And she wants to be here. So, let's go get you married. Yeah?"

I swallow—my throat dry and nod. I just need Dean and Hazel. They're my calming mechanisms. And they're both currently far away—down that long, long dirt and rose-petaled aisle. So—"Let's go!"

I step from the cabin door and the music changes. I am so ready for this. We've worked so hard to make this space delicate and elegant, ready for a wedding—it was already beautiful with the pines and aspens and forever sky. We just added some ribbon and tule, and a wooden arch—crafted by Dean—to marry beneath. That, and a bunch of white folding chairs for our guests to sit on. But I don't see any of our hard work. I don't make out any of the faces staring back at me.

I see Dean. And only Dean.

Black suit. Black Converse. And the biggest smile that's ever adorned his face. He is everything I need and everything I want all rolled into one. I will forever be thankful to Shelia for marrying my big dumb ex and putting my path in Dean's once more.

Though—I think we would have found each other anyway. I think the Universe knew that he was meant for me. And me for him. She would have found another way to bring us together. Because we are two of those fortunate people who are actually meant to be.

How did I get so lucky?

My eyes fill, making the world swirl behind a glassy wall. Dad kisses my cheek, the reverend says *something* to him—I'm not sure what, I'm not listening—and then, he's gone. He must be in his seat. At least I'm assuming he is.

But I wouldn't know.

My eyes are on Dean.

My mind is on Dean.

My heart is ready.

Beside me, Ebony reaches for my bouquet, and Dean

slips his hands into mine. One tear spills over and it's instinct. I calm my nerves by reaching up on my toes, giving Dean a soft kiss.

"Jumping the gun a bit, aren't we, Iris?" says Faith—the reverend we asked to marry us.

A rumble of laughter sounds from the audience—reminding me that we are far from alone.

Dean smiles down at me—he doesn't mind. Hazel sits beside him, nudging her curly-haired head into his leg. She wants in on the loving. I can't blame her. I squeeze one of Dean's hands, then drop it to give Hazel a head pat, before returning my hand to his.

"Ready?" Faith says—she's been talking. Again. *Whew.* I am going to struggle seeing or hearing anything, but Dean today.

I give her a nod. I'm not trying to be distracted.

"Paulo Coelhoe said, *When we love,*" Faith's tone is regal, "*we always strive to become better than we are. When we strive to become better than we are, everything around us becomes better too.* Iris." She nods at me. "Dean. You have loved deeply and have the chance to make everything—"

"Hmm-aughh," a whimper sounds next to me.

Faith pauses—we all pause. Even the trees around us have hushed to listen.

I turn to see Ebony beside me, face contorted—yet somehow she's smiling.

"Eb?" I whisper. I look from my sister to Yara—who is filming the whole thing of course. How could I ever forget that we are not alone?

And then a *wail* sounds from Beth. Every eye in the vicinity shifts to my friend. I've never seen Beth cry before and it is not pretty.

"I'm so sorry," she cries through her sobs—though no tears streak her face. "It's all so beautiful. Please continue." She waves us on.

I blink—officially woken up—then turn back to Dean.

His brow pinches, trying to return to where we are. I know—I'm doing the same thing. I take a breath and peer across from me.

He's here.

We're together.

This is our day.

And I'm back in that blissful place.

THIRTEEN

Beth

Beneath the folds of our skirts, I give Ebony my hand. There's sweat beading on her brow and Jet will not take his suspicious eyes off her. He knows— or at least he knows something is amiss.

"Let's begin again," Faith says, giving me the side-eye.

Sorry lady—that sob was necessary. I made a promise! I am the official wedding deflector! And I will not let my girl down.

Faith clears her throat. "You have made everything around you better, simply by loving one another." Faith smiles at Iris, then Dean. But I think she's watching me in her peripheral. She doesn't trust me—with good reason.

I keep my head forward, my eyes darting from Jet to Ebony to Tate—my husband looks at me as if I've gone crazy. He knew I was crazy when he married me! And he knows my job is the deflector! So, stop looking at me like that, Tate Wilhelm.

I'm distracted and I'm focused all at once. Man, I am so good. I can multi-task every bit as well as Ebony.

Until Faith says, "I understand you've written your own vows?"

Iris, as beautiful as the mountain scenery, nods. But Ebony's grip on my palm tightens. "Beth," she whispers so softly that if I weren't paying so close attention to her, I wouldn't have heard my name.

I study her—my eyes asking, *What?*

She blinks, her eyes darting down then back again—as if she were pointing down at herself.

And that's when I see it. The small damp spot on the front of Ebony's dress, growing larger by the second.

And then, I hear it. There's no whooshing. There's no flooding. Hollywood has lied to every pregnant woman in the world.

There's simply a trickle. But I'm pretty sure that Ebony is not peeing her pants—or her bridesmaid dress—in this moment.

She whimpers, holding in her cry. Her failure.

Hold off on that defeat, baby! Because we are not beaten. Not yet. Coco hasn't noticed and we're so close. So very close.

Until—"Ebony?" Jet can't keep his mouth shut. Did he seriously just interrupt Dean at the start of his wedding vow? Timing, man!

Iris's wildflower bouquet slips from Ebony's grasp, falling to the dirty ground. She lets out an audible moan, this one louder than the last.

So of course, as the official deflector—I join her. "Ahhh," I groan, once again grabbing the attention of every breathing being at this wedding. Everyone, but Jet. But then, that kid has only ever had eyes for Ebony.

Iris turns about, facing her misbehaving wedding line. We've been misbehaving all day.

"Ebony!" She squeaks, her palm pressed to her mouth. Her yelp has shifted everyone's attention away from me and right back onto Ebony.

Seriously, does no one respect my job?

"Whew!" I bark. "I could not hold that in." I swallow. "Too much water. I drank so much." I fan myself with my hand and sidestep so that I'm closer to Ebony and halfway over the wet trail she's leaving in the dirt.

"Your water—your water broke." Iris's hands shake in mid-air. She whips her head back to her waiting groom as if to ask if he is seeing this too.

"This ceremony is so much better than I thought it would be," Yara mutters to her assistant. They stand to the side, filming the entire scene—*live*—Yara's camera right on Ebony.

"Sweetheart?" Mrs. McCoy says, standing with her husband in the audience, her eyes on Ebony.

Jet hurries over—not caring that this is a wedding ceremony. He wraps one arm around her. There's a wrinkle across the middle of his forehead that will likely be there forever if he doesn't smooth it out soon.

"Time to go," Coco says, lifting her blue skirt.

"Stop it! All of you!" Ebony yells. She puffs out a breath, holding onto Jet's side. And while she's clearly in pain, her voice is loud and clear. "I did not hide labor pains all day long to miss this wedding." She gives one confident nod— toward Faith. "Proceed."

"Ebony," Jet says, his tone a whole lot like a librarian

scolding a kid for bringing back a book that's been ripped to shreds.

"No, Jet. We will head to the hospital when the wedding is over." Her fingers grabble at the front of his dress shirt. She fists a handful of material, untucking the shirt tail in the process. She's staying in this wedding line, and Jet isn't leaving her side.

"Ahh—" Jet looks from Ebony to me.

Which makes sense, I am running this heist. Right? "All right, Faith, could we possibly skip the vows? For now?"

The reverend blinks, her eyes finally landing on the bride and groom.

"I think that would be best," Dean says.

I clap my hands like I'm in charge of this whole shindig —you know, the wedding that Iris worked night and day on for months. "All right people, in your seats. Let's get this show on the road!"

Two whole minutes later, Dean is pecking his bride and Iris is one married lady.

Ebony is no longer hiding her labor face or groans. Everything is out now.

Yara grins as she peers down at her device. "That was outstanding," says the pretty dark-haired woman. She looks at her assistant, pointing to something she's watching. Ebony and I just gave her the show of a lifetime—*live*.

FOURTEEN

Ebony

"I s this why I wasn't allowed to look at the bride or Ebony?" Jet has one arm wrapped around my waist, shuffling me off to his Bronco as he grumps at Beth. "Why did I believe either of you? I knew something wasn't right. Yet, I went along like an idiot."

"Can we please discuss your idiocy later? Please!" I bark.

Beth shuffles behind us. "I'm sorry, Jet! I promised her. We couldn't let Iris down."

"Oh, don't blame this on Iris!" Iris's voice sounds behind us. I peer back, my sister has the skirts of her dress balled up and she's charging close behind. You'd think she'd be slow in a wedding dress, but the girl's also wearing white Converse tennis shoes and she's quite spry.

"I'm not blaming you, Iris. We just didn't want anything to ruin your day."

"What about my niece?" Iris barks, hands flaring as she loses her hold on her dress.

"Or nephew," my brand new brother-in-law and I say in unison.

With help from Jet, I slide onto the leather seat of Jet's car. A cross between pressure and someone attempting to rip my body in half overcomes me. "Can we discuss my idiocy later too? Please? Please!" Now that it's time to go—I'd really like to get there.

"We can and we will," Iris says. "*Later.*

She opens the back door to Jet's car—my passenger door still ajar—and climbs inside. "Let's go, Dean. She's your sister too now and she's not giving birth without us." Iris slams her door closed—ready to go as if she were the one giving birth today.

Jet shuts the door after me. He and Dean race around the vehicle—like an old TV show I used to watch with my grandpa, I almost expect someone to slide across the hood of the car.

"I'm sorry, Iris."

"Oh, be quiet," she says, whipping her veil out of her eyes.

Jet and Dean are like synchronized swimmers, opening their doors together and slamming them closed at the same moment.

I watch out my window, Beth and Coco, stand together, hand in hand, watching as we pull away. I watch them in my rearview mirror. Coco waves goodbye and then Bethany is yelling something, she claps her hands, and then—she's out of sight. I don't know what she's said or who she's signaling to or what scheme she has going, but she's up to something.

I whimper as another contraction hits. This wave is so much stronger and heavier than the last. Apparently, broken water equals a whole lot more pain.

"Oh, Ebony," Iris snakes her arm around my seat and chest, giving me a half hug from the backseat. "If I didn't love you so much, I'd kill you right now."

"Same," Jet says, eyes on the road. "I'd like to echo that."

"I know." My voice comes out with a cry and I really *really* hate the sound of it. I better return to normal once I have this baby. My hormones need to be put in check. No more crying, stupid hormones—got it? "I'm sorry. But you'd worked so hard for today. You'd made everything so special. I couldn't do that to you."

Iris sighs and hugs me tighter.

"Well," Dean says, "you did take the attention off of Iris with that live video. That's a wedding gift in itself."

A delirious laugh bubbles from my throat—I just had my water break and my best friend claim it as urine in front of eighty-seven thousand people. *Fantastic.*

"What's your vote, Dean?" I ask in an attempt to distract myself.

"My vote?"

"For the baby's gender. Everyone has one. What's yours?"

"Girl, like me," Iris says.

Just as Dean says, "Boy."

Another laugh bubble up—it's accompanied by a wave of tears. Stupid tears!

"Boy?" Iris says, taking her attention from me for only a second.

Dean lifts one shoulder, I have a better visual of him than my bride sister. "When you asked the first time I wasn't sure. I needed to feel things out a bit. I'm going with Ebony. Boy."

"You're sucking up to the woman in labor," Iris says—I can't tell if she's scolding Dean or laughing. If only I could see her face.

Dean laughs, a smile on his handsome face. I mean, he's no Jet Jacobson, but he's a cutie. "I'm not sucking up. I'm just getting boy vibes."

I hear the roll in my sister's eyes. "Boy vibes?"

"Please don't have your very first married argument three minutes after you've been wed, over my unborn child."

"Oh no," Jet says, taking a left turn, smooth and easy—though I can see he's driving twelve miles over the speed limit. "Save that for when Iris is pregnant and decides to hide the fact that she's in labor."

"I'm sorry, Jet. But I knew you'd make me go to the hospital."

Without looking my way, Jet slips the fingers on his right hand through my left. "You're absolutely right, I would have." He leans over, eyes on the mountain road, and kisses my fingers, before taking the wheel with both hands once more.

His sweet touch only brings on more tears. Dang you, Jet Jacobson. I never cried before Jet. But I love that man so much, I can't keep the tears at bay. They have a mind of their own.

I see a paved road up ahead and everyone else sees it too. It feels like the four of us take an audible breath together.

"Should I type in the fastest route to the hospital from here?" Dean asks, holding up his phone.

"I know the fastest route." Jet turns down a side street, the traffic minimal. "I figured it out a week ago."

"You did?" I say, my eyes watering.

"Of course I did." Jet shakes his head. "I can't carry the baby for you. I can't go through labor pains or morning sickness for you. I can't even gain weight for you. I am pretty much stuck rubbing your feet—which I don't mind, by the way—and calculating the fastest route to the hospital. However, I'm only allowed to complete that job when I'm made aware that my wife is in labor."

I sniff and run the back of my hand beneath my nose. I can hardly see with the never-ending tears. "You do so much more than that. And your foot rubs are magical. I can't do this without you. You know that, right?"

A sigh falls from Jet's chest. "I do. So, from now on—I get to be informed. Okay?"

I don't even argue. My instinct is to debate and figure out why I'm right and he is wrong. But I can't. He isn't wrong. And he's the best man I've ever known. So, I swallow my pride, clench with the oncoming contraction, and agree, "Okay."

"I see the hospital," Dean says, pointing from the back seat.

Another pain hits—this baby is coming. But at least he won't be born in the back of Jet's Bronco.

FIFTEEN

Coco

I lean my head on Jude's shoulder. Alice sits on his lap, her fingers lacing in and out of mine. She heaves a giant six-year-old sigh, her huff so big her bangs lift in flight. Maybe waiting at the hospital wasn't the best idea for Alice. But she insisted on coming.

"Making a baby sure takes a long time."

Jude gives me a sideways glance, a smirk playing at his lips.

"It does," I tell her. "But their baby is all made. It just needs to make it out into the world now."

"Ebony should consider herself lucky. She's only got one in there." She twists her little blonde head so that she's peering up at me. "Princess's mom had like a hundred babies all at the same time. It must have taken two years to get them all out."

"Well," I say, squinting down at my little stepdaughter. "Maybe not a hundred puppies."

"Oof," Beth plops into the seat opposite of where we sit in

this waiting room. Tate is already there and she sighs—a whole lot like my six-year-old—before tilting her head onto his shoulder. "Well, I'll tell you this. We are not having children."

"Yes we are," Tate says, winking at Alice.

She giggles and I feel the rumble of her laugh.

"No, we're not. If you want to be a father, then we'll adopt. But I am not doing *that*. "

"Birth is really beautiful, Beth. You'll change your mind." I *boop* Alice on the nose and give her a smile.

"Maybe when it's a llama. But a human woman should not have to do that."

I chuckle. "The experience is priceless and it's a labor of love. I promise you. My mom, Heidi," I clarify—since I have a birth and an adopted mother, "she would have given anything to have a baby."

Bethany swallows. She doesn't have any witty comebacks for that, it's too tender a topic.

I grin at her, attempting to bring back her humor. "Next time I've got an animal in labor, I'll invite you over to my clinic."

Beth croaks out a balking laugh. "Gee. Thanks."

"Will you have a baby?" Alice asks me. "Even though Ebony sounded like Princess that time I accidentally stepped on her tail?"

I clamp my teeth down on my bottom lip, my heart thumping harder. "I will."

"When? And will it be a sister? Because I am very opposed to the boy kind of babies. It's my baby too—so you should probably take that into consideration," she says, spitting out words that are much too old for her. "You should probably think about that."

I swallow, my stomach flipping.

"Boy babies are great. You'd like a boy baby, if you met one," Jude tells her.

She gives a little sixteen-year-old eye roll. "Yeah, well I guess we'll never know unless Coco gets cooking. When do you think you'll cook up a baby, Coco? Huh? When? Because enquiring minds would like to know."

"Well—" I start.

Jude peers down at her—giving her that face that I now know means, *please be polite.* "Alice, that might be a topic for—"

"Actually," I say, lifting my eyes to see Beth sit up a little taller—she's listening too. I ignore her and peer down at Alice, then up at Jude. "The answer to that question is sooner than you might think."

"Sooner!" Alice chimes. She presses her hands together and lifts her eyes to the ceiling. "Please let it be the girl kind! I promise to be the best big sister ever. But if it's the boy kind I can't promise a thing. Those are the rules. Sorry, Charlie."

"Sooner?" Jude says, brows knit.

"Sooner." I watch him, giving a slight nod.

"So are we cooking this girl up before Christmas?" Alice says, one of her little brows lowers with the question. "Because I'm a little concerned about Santa having to skimp on my toys. He knows I was here first, right? Do we need to write a letter?"

I clear my throat and take my eyes from my husband to my insanely smart six-year-old. "Nope. No letter. Not this year, Alice."

"Whew." She runs a little hand over her forehead. "Will

I still be six? Can you tell me that? Do we get any kind of timeline here, lady?"

"You'll be seven," I say, blinking from her to Jude. "But school will still be in session." I swallow, eyes on Jude. This isn't exactly how I'd planned to announce my pregnancy. I had suspicions, but I'd only confirmed them this afternoon. Not unlike Ebony, I waited to tell anyone, not wanting to take anything away from Iris's day.

"Coco Coalfield!"

"It's Taylor," I tell Beth. "Coco *Taylor*."

"Whatever," she says, both hands pinching the armrest of her chair. "You're pregnant?"

I let out a breathy laugh and peer up at Jude. "I am."

My husband presses a quick kiss to my mouth and when he releases me, there are tears on his cheeks.

"Woo! Hoo! Wait until I tell Grandma Lucy and Grandma Heidi and the Uncles." Alice giggles. "They are going to be more surprised than when Coco learned about my goodnight kisses with Sparkle Unicorn."

"Who?" Beth says, her head tilting.

More tears spill from Jude's eyes. His joy always seems to produce tears. "Ah, her beta fish."

Beth wrinkles her nose. "You kiss your fish goodnight?"

Alice sets a finger to her lips, then whispers, "I sure do. She needs all the loving she can get. But don't tell Coco. She disagrees."

"I can hear you, Alice."

Alice sighs. "Right. You've got those mom ears now." She twists her lips to the side. "Coco, I will promise to stop kissing Sparkle Unicorn, if you promise to make our baby the girl kind."

I can't muster the energy to be mad at her—plus, she

already promised to stop kissing Sparkle Unicorn "I don't get to choose, Alice. A baby is a gift and we don't get to choose what kind."

"So, like when Grandma Taylor gave me that blue shirt for my birthday? Ew. I wear pink and sparkles. Not blue. But we just smiled and said thanks because it was a gift. Hey, then Daddy let me go to the store and exchange it!" Her eyes brighten. "Will there be an exchange program?"

"Alice," Jude scolds—but that man has no idea how to sound stern. "Coco is right. A baby is a gift. And boy or girl, we'll love it." He presses a kiss to the top of her head. "You, young lady, will love him—"

"Or her," Alice says, "Coco is still cooking it up, Daddy."

"Or her," Jude agrees. "We'll talk about this later. Okay?"

"Okay," she says, leaning her head against my arm. "But just to play it safe Coco, I think you should wear pink from now on. And Iris's Gramgram could bedazzle a few things for you. She's bedazzling a bunch for me. She's pretty fabulous."

I sigh. "Good idea, Alice." But my eyes are on Jude.

Tears still swim, glassing over his vision. "I love you," he mouths to me, pressing another kiss to my lips before I can return the sentiment.

SIXTEEN

Iris

I pace outside my sister's hospital room door, my wedding gown dragging on the ground.

"Sweetheart, maybe you and Dean should go sit," Mom says.

I shake my head. "We aren't going anywhere."

"These things can take time."

"They sure can," Gramgram says, her large bosom swaying along with her hips. "I might go find Frank. Did he come to the hospital?"

"Mom," my mother moans.

"He's got Johnny on vinyl, dear. I can't resist."

Beth's granddad did come with her. And I'm pretty sure he was nuzzling on my Gramgram's ear earlier. I thought I saw the two of them in the cabin before the ceremony.

Gramgram shuffles off, her long muumuu dress swaying as she goes.

"Dear, you should sit." My mother rubs her hands together.

But I don't want to sit. I don't want to miss a thing.

"Barb," Dean says to Mom, "do you need a drink? We could take a walk and go grab one?"

Mom sets her palm on Dean's cheek. "I always wanted a son. I'm so glad I have the two sweetest sons-in-law." She gives Dean's cheek a pat. "I'll get the drinks, you get Iris to sit down."

Mom trots down the hallway, stopping to stare at where Gramgram went into the waiting room to find Frank.

"I don't want to sit," I tell my brand-new husband.

"I know. You don't have to. I was just trying to redirect her."

"I know. And thank you." I reach up on my toes and press a kiss to his lips. Dean snakes one arm about my waist.

"I love you, Iris Hale."

Despite the stress, I can't help but beam. *Iris Hale.* I love the sound of that.

"Ooo a wedding? Did you come from a wedding?" A nurse walking by stops next to us.

Dean lifts one shoulder. "Nah, I just enjoy wearing a tux." He's a regular comedian.

I snicker and wrap one arm around Dean's neck. "Yes, we *just* got married. My sister is having her baby. So, now, we're here."

"We didn't even make it to our own reception." Dean laughs.

Before the girl can respond, Yara taps the nurse on the shoulder. Where did she come from? What is she doing here? I assumed she'd left. The wedding is over. We did not agree to an Instagram live birth.

Yara and the nurse walk away—the same direction the nurse came from. Mom is back too, stopping to chat with

Yara and the nurse along her way. She's got a drink in each hand but she's more focused on talking than the sodas she carries. I don't have the energy to worry about what my mother might be saying to the social media influencer.

"I wonder how long this is going to take." I lean my head on Dean's chest, listening to his heartbeat.

"I don't know. Can I do anything for you?"

"Let's see," I say, peering up at him. "You already married me—so yeah, I think we're good."

We stand there half an hour longer and I'm thinking maybe we should pull up a couple of chairs when Mom returns—she ended up going back into the waiting room. And her drinks are missing. I've just been over here stewing —not sitting and not drinking.

"Sweetheart, can I see you and Dean for a minute?"

I nibble on my lip. I really don't want to go too far. "Ah—"

"Just around the corner. We'll be close if our baby decides to make an appearance." She gives me a crinkle-nose smile. This *is* her first grandbaby, I'm guessing she wants to be close by just as badly as I do.

"Sure," I say, finding my compassion. Ebony says it's my superpower—and it does come easily.

My shoes pad along the hard ground and once again I am thankful for my Converse. I can't imagine standing this long in high heels.

We follow her down the hall and around the corner to the waiting room where Beth, Coco, and the others have been. I walked by this room earlier—I'm pretty sure it didn't have pink and blue streamers swooping from one wall to the other the first time. The chairs have all been pushed to the side and in the center of the room there is a pink tissue ball pom pom hanging from the ceiling.

I'm lost. "What's happening?" I say to no one in particular.

"Ahh… baby celebration?" Dean guesses.

Yara stands in the corner, her phone out, with our friends and family at the edges of the room, their eyes all on us.

"I… don't… think so."

"It's a dance!" Alice jumps in the air, holding out her arms like a game show model.

"A *first* dance," Coco says as we walk past her, "as husband and wife."

Gramgram stands between Coco and Frank. "If that little peanut doesn't hurry up we'll miss the entire reception."

A soft ballad starts to play and I look over at Dean—his eyes sparkle and he's glowing as he peers around the waiting room. His expression tells me he didn't plan this.

"I told your mother I had the perfect Johnny song, but she wouldn't listen."

I cinch my brows together, a laugh bubbling from my chest.

For the next five minutes, I dance with my Dean, peering up into his sapphire eyes. I ignore the phone Yara has pointed our direction and listen to the rhythm of the music—it lulls me. It calms me. It reminds me that today will forever be meaningful, in so many ways.

"We got married today," Dean says.

"Did you almost miss it?"

"Between your sister going into labor and Beth sobbing —yeah, I almost did."

"Whew," I fake relief. "I'm so glad you didn't."

"I'm sorry about the wedding you planned, Iris. It was beautiful. And the reception—"

I shake my head. We may never see the reception hall that I meticulously chose, and prepped, and decorated. But I don't care. There's no other place I'd rather be. Ebony's baby is coming, Dean is at my side, and I am a married to my best friend, next to Hazel, of course.

SEVENTEEN

Beth

When the second song begins, I wink at Tate and slip out the door. That man is a trooper. I'm thankful for the Converse Iris made us all wear —that means I don't even have to remove my shoes while sneaking down this hospital hallway.

Sure, there may be locked doors with nurses coming and going, but I'm patient. I am laser-focused, a leopard tracking its prey.

I wait until the nurses behind the desk are distracted and another uses her keycard to open the locked double doors. The ones only Iris, Dean, and the rest of the "family" were allowed through.

Come on, people. Ebony and I are as family as you can get. Sure, we don't share the same blood, but I have eaten her nasty chocolate cake multiple times, all because she and I are like family.

Once the nurse opens the locked doors and walks through, I slip in behind her. *Success*! And because I'm a leopard who pays attention—and I've been planning this heist all along—I know that Ebony is in room 46A.

I tug on the silver handle of her door, happy to find it isn't locked.

The room is dim and quiet—there isn't nearly the moaning and yelling down this hallway that I expected.

I slink against the wall, head down, and tip-toe more fully into the room.

Jet dabs at Ebony's head with a cloth. My friend is now in a hospital gown, her pretty chiffon dress discarded to the unused chair behind Jet. I have a side-view of Ebony—in *stirrups. Yikes.* A doctor sits at the end of her bed, ready to play catcher.

That's when a small queasiness begins to stir in my stomach. I set a palm to my abdomen. I'm not pregnant, am I? This isn't morning sickness, right? *No*—it's not like I could have caught it from Ebony or Coco. Tate and I have been careful. Very careful.

Still, the queasiness in my gut won't cease.

I am *not* pregnant.

I'm not.

But seeing Ebony in that bed, feet in the stirrups—*oof*—it does not sit well with my very unpregnant self.

"Are we ready to push?" The umpire at Ebony's feet asks.

Pushing? Already? No! I just came in for a quick hug and hello. I just wanted to check on her. I did not come here to see the action.

I could just slip right out those doors and no one would ever know that I even entered them.

But it's Ebony. How can I not check on her?

I'm pondering. I'm weighing all the pros and cons—just like Iris would—all while I slink farther into this room.

In fact, I'm pondering and weighing so much that I don't see the tray of tools right directly next to me. Not until I slink into them and they spill across the tiled floor.

"Beth?" Ebony squeaks, while everyone else in the room has gone quiet.

"Who is this person?" One of the nurses asks.

"Ah, I'm the best friend. Her maid of honor—or at least I would have been, had she had one. I—"

"You need to leave," the same nurse gripes.

But before I can argue why I should get to stay—even though I'm not really sure that I *want* to stay—Ebony lets out a loud groan.

See—*that's* what I thought this section of the hospital would sound like.

"He's coming!" Ebony moans.

"Or *she*," I say—only to be laden with a glare from Nurse Panties-In-A-Bunch. "Well, we don't know for certain, and my vote is girl."

"Bethany!" Ebony cries. And I'm not sure if that tone means I should stay or go. But then, her right arm flails out, her fingers wagging. I feel like that's a *come here* sign.

So, I ignore Nurse Panties and leave the safety of the wall. I grab a hold of Ebony's right hand, while Jet has her left.

"You've got his, Ebony," he tells her.

Her hands around ours go stark white, with the tips of her fingers turning a bright pink.

"Ouch," I whisper—which, sure in retrospect, might be the wrong time to tell her that she's breaking my pinky finger.

"That's it, Ebony," says the umpire. "I've got shoulders. One more big push."

"Shoulders?" I can't decide if I want to peek or pass out.

Ebony's face goes red and Jet pushes back more straight chestnut hairs from her sweaty face.

Yep—adoption, all the way.

And then, someone is crying. A tiny, goopy someone, still attached to my best friend.

The umpire doctor sets the little person right on Ebony's chest. "It's a boy," he says with a grin.

Ebony sighs, breathless. "My little soccer man." Her eyes glisten as she peers down at her son. "Told ya," she sighs, breathless. Her tired eyes slide from Jet to me.

Jet Jacobson—pro athlete—has tears streaming down his cheeks, and a smile the size of Texas on his face.

And while I'm loving every second of this moment—the queasiness has been replaced with the greatest high I've ever experienced—I'm also intruding.

So, just as I slinked my way in, I take one more glance at Ebony and her sweet little family, then slink my way out.

My nose runs and tears blur my vision. Ebony is a mama. She and Jet have a son! *A son.*

I run now, not caring that I can't see or that Nurse Panties-In-A-Bunch has friends who are picking up their phones and surely calling security on me. I push through the double doors—thankful they aren't locked from this side—and race down to where the rest of our party is celebrating.

"He's here!" I yell, bursting through the waiting room entrance. "It's a boy and he is here!"

EIGHTEEN

Ebony

A lot is going on—with the doctor and nurses, with the baby, with me. But my eyes follow the little man who, in an instant, has completely stolen my heart. Even quicker than his dad.

They clean him up on a small table at my left. And while Jet goes from me to the baby and back again, my eyes stay glued to that tiny pink person.

It feels like an eternity before they set him, bundled in a blanket, back in my arms. I know they have to take him back for a more thorough bathing and testing, but I'm not ready. We've been inseparable for months and I can't stand the thought of him not being right next to me.

"We'll give you a minute," says Nurse Kailey, who I thought might eat Bethany alive earlier. She lays baby boy in my arms and gives me a small wink. Doctor John has already finished with me. He's off with a promise to return and check on us later. The rest of the team takes their time, doing what they need to, but then they leave too. And we are given a gift, a moment, just the three of us.

Jet sniffles. "I've only thought of girl names."

I chuckle—and it isn't comfortable. Ouch. I didn't make it in time for an epidural. And I am feeling it. *Nothing* is numb. "I know. You should have trusted me."

"You're right. You are always right."

"Now stitch that on a pillowcase and we've got décor for the bedroom."

Jet hunches, standing next to me, but leaning over to press a kiss to our little son's head. A teardrop falls onto the blue blanket they've wrapped him in.

"Who's emotional now?" I say, but I can't blame him. Our boy is perfection with Jet's dark hair and eyes as blue as Iris's—though the books say his eyes may change. Tenth-grade biology tells me they *will* change with Jet and I both being brown-eyed.

"Look at his fingers, Eb, they're so long."

"You're going to wake him up," I say, but I can't help but smile. I'd like to see his eyes again, anyway. We only got a quick glimpse right after I delivered.

"So," Jet's gaze slides to mine, "do *you* have a name?"

"I've thought of a few." We spent so much time arguing over the baby's gender—we never made it around to a name discussion.

"And? Are you going to be tight-lipped about this too?"

"Am I ever going to be forgiven?" I feign a giant smile.

"Sure. As soon as he turns ten."

I chortle but moan with the ache it causes. "*Jet.*"

"You're forgiven. As long as you never do anything like that to me again." He straightens and peers down at our son. "Can I?"

I nod. "Yes. Take him."

Jet does and our little man—who I am secretly calling Nox—looks so tiny in Jet's massive arms. "So, names? We can't call him *little man* forever."

"How about Peanut?"

Jet gently bounces, moving his entire body with the motion. "Not even peanut."

I swallow. "I've been thinking about *our* names and what might represent us both."

"Like a ship name? *Jeb?*" Jet wrinkles his nose. "You just don't look like a Jeb," he says to our baby.

I giggle, watching the two of them and feeling as if I may burst with the strangest, most indescribable joy. "No. Not Jeb. Something like Cole. Or… *Nox*."

"Aw. I get it. Ebony, Jet—something black."

"Kind of. Nox means night. I thought it fit."

"Nox," Jet says and I love the way it sounds on his lips and in his deep tone. "*Nox*. I like it."

"Yeah?"

"Yeah."

"What do you think?" he says to the baby. "Do you like it?" He peers up to me. "I think he likes it."

"Are you going to be this easy with all of our life decisions?" I ask him.

"That depends. Are you there? If so, then I'm probably in." He leans down, holding little Nox between us and pressing a sweet kiss to my lips.

"I love you, Jet Jacobson."

There's a tap on the door, Iris pushes her way inside—wedding dress and all. The girl hasn't changed yet.

"Hello?" she says, tentatively. Mom, Dad, Dean, and Gramgram are close behind her.

"I said family first!" I hear Nurse Kailey say.

"I told you. I *am* family! Practically." And that would be my Beth.

She doesn't make it through the door this time, so, I'm assuming that Nurse Kailey won this round. Poor Beth.

"A boy?" Iris says, her eyes on me. She's as surprised as Jet.

"A boy," I tell her—and yes, maybe I use a tone that says, *how could you doubt me*, but I was right!

"Do you want to hold him?" Jet asks my sister. "Ah—as long as that's okay with Grandma," he says, quickly back-tracking.

"Of course—my special wedding gift to Iris." Mom nods and Iris steps over to where I lay and Jet stands with our little man.

"Nox," Jet says and Iris blinks up at him, "this is your Aunt Iris. It's her wedding day, so maybe don't pee on her just yet."

Iris chokes on a half hiccup, half laugh, and holds out her arms for little Nox. Jet settles the baby in her arms— already the pro-Dad. He snaps a picture of the two of them and each member of my family after.

It's surreal and beautiful, and completely exhausting.

NINETEEN

Coco

A lice stands on a chair next to me and we watch through this nursery window as the nurse bathes and dresses little Nox. We haven't officially met him yet, but Alice and I are enjoying the view.

"He's pink."

"He is kind of pink, isn't he?"

"Are we sure he's a boy?" she huffs out a breath and wrinkles her little nose, thinking.

"We're sure," I tell her.

She sets both of her palms to the window, nose pressed to the glass as she takes a closer look. "I think I'd like some proof." Her little blonde head whirls around to look at me, she pokes me in the belly. "Hey!" She points to a baby behind the glass. "If that one is a boy, then there must be more girls to pass out! Maybe we *will* get a girl. I am going to start wishing on every star that all the other mommies have boys! Then we will for sure get the girl kind."

My brows knit and I can't help but smile at her logic. "I'm not sure it works like that, Alice."

She inhales a big breath, then sighs. "It does. Trust me."

"Hey look, he's getting a hat."

Alice giggles. "I still want the girl kind. But Daddy was right. I like the boy kind too. When can I hold him?"

"We'll have to talk to Ebony about that."

"Oh, Ebony will let me. She said she'd give me whatever I wanted if I never asked her again how that baby got inside her belly. Besides, Gramgram told me she'd let me hold the baby before even her, on account of I found her and Granddad Frank in a closet looking for contact lenses. At least that's what Gramgram said, but they both wear glasses so I don't think that crazy lady knows what the heck she's talking about. But I told her I wouldn't mention that sight to a soul. So, I get to go before even crazy Gramgram."

"Hey, don't call Gramgram crazy. That isn't nice."

"But did you hear what I said—they both had glasses on."

I shift—actually thinking about what she's said. "Even still, please don't call our friends crazy. It's rude."

"Yes, Momma."

I freeze in place, my heart stopping with her words.

Then Alice presses all five of her fingers to her face—giving herself a miss piggy nose. She giggles and giggles. Finally, she speaks. "I meant, Coco." She shakes her head as if her slip-up was the silliest thing in the world.

But I could cry—tears of joy.

I won't ever try to replace or be Sandra.

But I do love my little Alice. I love her like I've never loved another human. She's mine. We *are* family. And while she's praying for the baby vending machine to spit out a girl for us. I'll be praying that she slips up on my name again and again, until one day Momma just sticks.

The nurse sees us watching and brings baby Nox over to the glass. She holds him up for us to see and a tear slips down my cheek.

Alice slips her little hand into mine. "It's okay, Coco. I'm sure our baby will be the girl kind."

TWENTY

Iris

It's another two and a half hours before Dean can convince me it's time to leave the hospital. Beth, Coco, Mom, Dad, Gramgram, and Frank have all moved on to our wedding reception. They're waiting for us.

Technically, we have the hall the whole night, so I guess we can extend the celebration time.

When Dean misses the turn to the hall and keeps going up the mountain toward the cabin we rented, I speak up. "The turn," I point, thinking how Hazel will be at the reception hall, missing me. She stayed with my cousins while we ran to the hospital and I'm sure she hated every minute of it. At least Travis didn't come.

"Did I miss it?" he says, but he's smiling—that smile I fell in love with more than a year ago.

"Dean?"

"I just forgot something at the cabin. Don't worry about Hazel, she's with Coco and Alice now."

It's like he's read my mind. "What did you forget?"

"Iris," he says, eyes sliding from the road to my face.

I sigh. Clearly, he has something up his sleeve and I shouldn't spoil it. "Okay."

I'm not sure what I expect, a party, or a welcome committee, but the cabin is cleared of everyone. Maybe he did forget something. There's a light on at the front deck and my eyes draw to the light—no, *lights*. There's a row of twinkle lights lining the deck rail.

Dean stops in front of the cabin and kills the engine. The twinkle lights shine bright now that the sun has gone down. He slips from the car and jogs around to open my passenger door.

"What are we doing?"

He holds out a hand and I take it, stepping from the car out onto the dirt floor. My long dress falls to the ground, nature's floor, covered in dirt and leaves.

"Are we going to make it to the reception?" I ask.

He lifts one shoulder. "That's up to you." He squeezes my fingers and leads me up the cabin steps and around to the deck where there are not only twinkle lights and stars lighting up the space, but two plush love-sacs, one beside the other. There's a platter with meat, cheese, and crackers and a bottle of wine with two waiting glasses on a blanket in front of the two overstuffed pillows. "I never got to give you my vows."

"Your vows?" My throat tightens.

"Yes. My vows. Why not now? And here? It's still our wedding day. I don't need an audience, or Yara, or thousands of strangers watching me to say them. I just need you." He leans down, brushing a soft kiss to my lips and filling my chest with fireworks.

Tears brim in my eyes. "That sounds perfect."

Dean walks me over to one of the love-sacs and I sit, my big dress poofing out around me. He screws in the cork and removes the lid from the long-neck bottle, filling the two glasses, then passing one over to me before taking the seat right next to me.

I breathe in the autumn night and the nature around us. It's cool out tonight and yet Dean is keeping me warm.

Dean pulls his phone from his jacket pocket, tapping on the screen until he's pulled up exactly what he wants. "Iris," he starts, and already a tear leaks from my eye. He breathes out a laugh and swipes it from my cheek with the pad of his thumb. "No crying, Iris McCoy. No crying."

"*Hale*," I remind him. "Iris Hale."

He nods, pulls in a breath, and starts again. "Iris, in a way I have always loved you. You were the girl who offered me a smile and a kind word when I was a lonely sixteen-year-old. You were the girl who made me laugh when I had nothing to laugh at. Fast forward a few years and suddenly you needed me. You needed a date and I came to your aid. You may have thought that I rescued you that night, but you saved me long before that."

I can't help the tears—despite his plea for me to stay dried-eyed.

"You are gifted, kind, and beautiful. You see the best in everyone and every situation. You make me a better man and this world a better place. I love you. I love Hazel. And one day, if I'm lucky enough, maybe I'll make Hazel status."

I smirk and about choke on my tears.

"Thank you for taking a chance on a fake date, and for letting me love you the rest of my life."

I blink, peering over at him. I lift my shoulder with one single shrug—as if to silently say, *I can't help it.* These tears are all his fault, not mine. I lean and Dean meets me halfway with a kiss.

My vows will have to wait, our friends and family will have to wait, even my Hazel baby will have to wait. I'm kissing my new husband. And I don't plan to stop for a very long time.

Acknowledgments

Short & sweet. Like this book.

Gosh, HUGE thank you to everyone who has loved and supported this series.

I love you back!

It's been such a joy to create these characters who, at this point, feel a whole lot like friends.

Thank YOU for helping me make them into something special!

xoxo,

Jen

About the Author

Jen Atkinson has been dreaming up love stories and writing them down since she learned her ABCs in elementary school. While Jen has written a variety of genres, from romantic suspense to laugh out loud romcoms, all of her novels contain three things: a love story, a happily ever after, and all are sweet reads! If you want to feel all the feels, and get a little light head from swooning over cinnamon roll heroes, grab one of Jen's books.

Made in the USA
Columbia, SC
04 October 2023

23857856R00064